TIPPLE ROAD

MICHAEL OCHOTORENA

Tipple Road
By **Michael Ochotorena**

Burning Bulb Publishing
P.O. Box 4721
Bridgeport, WV 26330-4721
United States of America
www.BurningBulbPublishing.com

PUBLISHER'S NOTE: This book is a work of fiction. Names, characters, places, and incidents are either the product of the author's imagination or are used fictitiously, and any resemblance to actual persons, living or dead, events, or locales is purely coincidental.

First Edition.

Paperback Edition ISBN: 978-1-964172-61-3

Dedicated to Cece–
my real life Annabeth, who helped me find the Lord
and brought my heart back to life again.

Chapter One

A Boy Without a Father

Listen. Before I tell you how it ended, I gotta tell you how it started, because the end don't make sense unless you got the beginning. And the beginning is a kid. Skinny brown kid, too-big T-shirt, knees scraped to hell, sitting on the curb on a side street off Pico Boulevard waiting for a man who ain't coming. That's me. That's Miguel. Six years old and already learning what nobody is supposed to teach a child that young — that some doors stay closed no matter how loud you knock.

My mother, God bless her, she did what she could. She worked two jobs and came home smelling like fryer grease and bleach, and she kissed the top of my head and told me bedtime stories in Spanish even when she was so tired she was falling asleep mid-sentence. Mi reina, that woman. Saint with cracked hands. But a mother can only fill so much of a hole, and the hole in a boy where his father is supposed to live — that hole is shaped like a man, and only a man fits inside it.

My father. Let me tell you about my father. He was handsome the way trouble is handsome, you know what I'm saying? Slick hair, gold tooth, voice like Sunday radio. He was the kind of man who could walk into a room and make every woman in it forget her own name, and that was his great talent in life — being forgotten by, and then forgetting. Drugs, mujeres, the party that never ends. He chose the party over me about a thousand times before I was old enough to count to a thousand. Birthdays came and went. School plays. The Little League game where I hit a triple and stood on third base looking into the bleachers for a face that was never going to be there. I'd see other kids' fathers — pale, brown, black, didn't matter — clapping, hollering, hoisting their boys up on their shoulders like trophies. And I would stand on third base in the dust with my heart in my throat, and I would tell myself, no llores, Miguelito, no llores, only babies cry.

So I didn't cry. I did something worse. I got mad.

Anger is a strange currency. You don't notice it accumulating until one day you go to spend something else — kindness, patience, love — and you reach in your pocket and find nothing but anger in there. That's all you got. That's all you can pay with. So that's what you pay with.

By the time I was eleven I was paying with it everywhere. School, I paid with it. Some teacher tried to be nice to me, I read it as condescension and I paid her in attitude. Some kid bumped me in the hallway, I paid him in fists. The principal had my mother in his office so many times she stopped taking off her work apron when she came. She would just sit there in that orange Denny's apron with her hands folded and listen to a man tell her that her son was, quote, headed down a dark path, and she would nod, and her eyes would get wet but she wouldn't let the tears fall because she was a soldier, my mother, she was made of harder stuff than any of us.

The dark path. Funny how grown men love that phrase like they invented it. Like there's a lit path and a dark path and a kid just decides one morning over his cereal which one to walk down. Nah. The truth is, the dark path comes and finds you. It walks up to you on a hot afternoon when you're twelve years old and you're sitting on the same curb you sat on at six, still waiting for the same man, and it sits down next to you and says, oye, primo, you hungry? And you are. You are so hungry, and not just for food.

— ✦ —

His name was Casper. Twenty-two, maybe twenty-three years old, but to a twelve-year-old he was a god — a god in a white tee and creased Dickies, with a teardrop tatuaje under his eye that I would learn later he had not actually earned, but it didn't matter, because in that neighborhood the symbol was the thing. He bought me a torta. Carne asada, extra avocado, the kind my mother could not afford to buy me twice in a week. He watched me eat it with this little half-smile, like he was watching an investment mature.

"Tu papá," he said, "he around?"

I shook my head. Mouth full. Couldn't speak.

"Yeah," he said. "I know how that is. Mira, mijo. You ever need anything — anything — you come find me. You hear me? La familia, that's not the people whose blood you got. La familia, that's the people who show up."

And he showed up. That was his great trick, the one my real father had never learned. He showed up. He showed up at my school when some older kid was muscling me for my lunch money, and the older kid evaporated like a puddle in August. He showed up at my house with groceries when my mother had pneumonia and couldn't work a week. He showed up at the park to teach me how to throw a punch — fist tight, thumb outside, drive from the hip, papo, the hip — and he showed up at the corner store and bought me my first forty when I was thirteen and laughed when I made the face.

By the time I was old enough to understand what he was, I already loved him. That's the trap, see. They get you young and they get you with kindness, because cruelty only works on people who already have something to lose, and a boy with nothing — a boy with a hole shaped like a man — that boy is wide open. That boy will mistake the first hand that feeds him for the hand of God.

I jumped in at twelve. The beating took a minute and a half and felt like an hour and a half, and when it was over Casper picked me up off the asphalt and hugged me and said, you my brother now, mijo, and I cried. First time I'd cried since the third-base game, and I told myself it was because of the punches, but it wasn't. It was because somebody had finally said the word brother and meant it, and I didn't know yet that the price of that word was going to be every other word I ever wanted to be called. Son. Husband. Father. Friend.

All of those words were going to get traded in for that one word.

Brother.

Pretty good deal at twelve. You don't know what you're spending yet.

Chapter Two

The Soldier

You want to know how a kid becomes a man in the life? He doesn't. That's the joke. A man is something you grow into by years and weather and the love of women and the disappointment of fathers. In the life, you don't grow into a man, you skip the step entire. One day you're a kid, the next day you're a soldier, and the thing in between — the thing that should have happened, the slow becoming — you just lose it. It falls out of you like a tooth and you wake up one morning and run your tongue around your mouth and feel the gap where it used to be and you think, huh. Guess I'm done now.

By fifteen I was running packages. By sixteen I was running corners. By eighteen I had two strikes I'd beaten on technicalities thanks to a public defender who liked me because I read her copy of Bless Me, Ultima cover to cover while waiting on my arraignment and we had something to talk about. She told me, Miguel, you're a smart kid, you don't have to do this. And I looked at her — sweet white lady, fresh out of UCLA Law, idealistic as a baby duck — and I said, Yes I do, ma'am. Where I'm standing, this is the only door.

She didn't have an answer for that. They never do. People who weren't raised in it always think there's a door you just haven't noticed. But I'm telling you, there is no door. There's the wall, and there's the part of the wall that has been worn smooth by generations of brown shoulders pushing against it, and that smooth spot is what we call a door. It is not a door. It is just a part of the wall that has given up faster than the rest.

They moved me up because I had a head for it. Most of the homies were soldiers — fists and heart, pero la cabeza, the head, they didn't have it. Numbers slipped out of them like water through a colander. Me, I could hold a ledger in my mind. I could remember who owed what, who had paid, who was running short, who was lying. I never wrote anything down. Casper used to tap his temple and say, mi contador, mi pequeño contador. My little accountant.

So I was the accountant. And when the books didn't balance, I was the man they sent to balance them.

The first time, I was nineteen. Pendejo named Flaco owed eight hundred and had been ducking calls for three weeks. Casper handed me a Louisville Slugger and said, you don't gotta kill him, just remind him about gravity. I remember walking up the steps of Flaco's apartment in Boyle Heights at three in the morning. I remember the smell of cat piss in the hallway and the broken light fixture that buzzed on and off like a dying bee. I remember the sound my heart was making — not loud. Quiet. Quieter than it should have been. That's what scared me later, when I had time to think about it. How quiet it was. How easy.

Flaco answered the door in his boxers. He saw me, he saw the bat, and he started crying before I even said hello. Crying and saying mi bebé, mi bebé está durmiendo, please, the baby, the baby. And I'm gonna tell you what I did, because if I don't tell you the bad part you won't believe the good part later. I did not care. I heard him say baby and I felt nothing — not pity, not horror, not even the satisfaction of having power. I felt the same thing you feel when somebody tells you what they had for lunch. Nothing. A kind of fog. I told him to step into the hall, and he did, and I worked his ribs and his thigh and one elbow until he was on the linoleum gasping, and the whole time the only thought in my head was that the dying-bee light fixture was annoying me and somebody should fix it.

I left him eight hundred dollars lighter and one elbow weaker. I walked back down the steps. I drove home with the radio on a Spanish ballad station and I ate carnitas at a 24-hour spot at four in the morning and I slept like a baby. Like Flaco's baby, probably, in the next room over, who never woke up the whole time her father was being broken in the hall.

That's the part nobody tells you about. They tell you the violence is hard. The violence is not hard. The violence is easy. What is hard is the fog. The fog is what eats you. The fog is what eats you slow, like a cancer made of nothing, and one day you look up and you don't recognize what's left.

Women. You want me to tell you about women. There were many. I'll spare you the parade. Tall ones, short ones, pretty ones, sad ones, ones who knew exactly what I was and ones who told themselves stories about who I might become. None of them stayed past breakfast, and I never asked them to. I had a twisted notion in my head about what love was. Love, in my head, was the thing my father had walked away from. Love was the trap that closed on a man and made him weak. Love was the apron my mother wore in the principal's office. Love was a bill you could not pay.

So I did not pay it. I took what looked like love and I used it the way you use a paper towel — once, and then in the trash, and then the next one. I told myself I was being honest because I never lied to any of them about what I was. As if honesty about cruelty makes the cruelty less. It does not. It just makes you a man who is honest and cruel, which is, if anything, worse than a liar, because a liar at least believes in the shape of the better thing.

I did not believe in any better thing. I believed in cash, and the weight of a pistola in the small of my back, and the loyalty of homies who would die for me on a Tuesday and forget my name on a Wednesday, and that was the whole architecture of my heart. Four walls. No roof. No furniture inside.

I was twenty-six years old and already, secretly, in a place I did not have words for yet — already tired. Tired the way a man is tired when he has been carrying the same bucket up the same hill for fifteen years and the bucket has a hole in it and the hill never ends. I did not say it out loud. You don't say it out loud. Saying it out loud is how you end up in a ditch off the 605 with your tongue cut out. But I felt it, in the small hours, in the fog. Tired. Tired.

And then Casper called me into the back office of the carnicería where we did our talking, and he poured me a glass of Don Julio, and he said, Miguelito, mi contador, I got a job for you. A run. A small town. East. And I'm going to tell you, papo — when he said the words West Virginia, the first thing I thought, before anything else, was: Where the hell is that? And the second thing I thought was: I do not want to go.

I should have listened to that second thought. I never did, in those days. I never listened to anything that sounded like it was coming from inside me. I had spent fifteen years learning to drown that voice, and I was good at it. Champion swimmer in the drowning of voices, that's what I was.

But the voice was right. And in a way I would not understand for many weeks, the voice was already God. And God had bought me a one-way ticket to a place I had never heard of, and was waiting for me there, in a diner, in the shape of a woman.

Chapter Three

Eastbound

"No," I said.

Casper looked at me over the rim of his glass like I'd spoken a language he did not recognize. He set the glass down. Slow. Not angry — that was the scary thing about Casper, he did not get angry, he got slow. The slower he got, the closer somebody was to bleeding.

"No," he said. Tasting the word. "No, he says. Mi contador says no."

"Send Pelón," I said. "Send Travieso. Send anybody. I'm not built for that — driving cross-country into hillbilly country with a trunk full? That's not my lane, Casper. I'm a city dude. I get pulled over in Oklahoma I'm cooked, you know I'm cooked, I got that face, I got these tatuajes —"

"These tatuajes," he said, "that I paid for. These tatuajes that say you belong to me."

There it was. The slow.

He leaned forward. He put his hands flat on the desk, palms down, the way a priest puts his hands on an altar. "Mijo. Listen to me. Listen to me with your ears and not your mouth. I picked you up off the curb. I fed you. I taught you everything you know. When your mama got sick, who paid for her medicine? When you caught that case at seventeen, who paid the lawyer? When you needed a car to go to her funeral, whose Cadillac did you drive? I have been your father, Miguel. The only father you ever had. And now I am asking my son to do one thing for me. One thing. And my son is going to tell me no?"

He let it sit. The carnicería was quiet except for the hum of the meat case in the next room. I could smell the blood through the wall — old blood, fresh blood, the blood of every animal that had ever passed through that place. It smelled like my whole life.

"No," he said again, softly, "is not a word my son uses. My son says, sí, papá. When?"

I looked at him for a long second. I thought about my mother, who was four years in the ground. I thought about the Cadillac. I thought about the lawyer in her UCLA suit telling me there was a door. I thought about the fog.

“Sí, papá,” I said. “When?”

He smiled. He poured me another Don Julio. He told me Tuesday.

I left Los Angeles on a Sunday morning at four a.m. to beat the heat through the desert. Black F-150 with Texas plates that did not belong to anybody whose name I knew. The product was where the product is always: not where you'd look first, not where you'd look second, somewhere they would only find on the third pass, by which time you are supposed to already be talking your way out of it or running. I had a burner phone, a clean ID that said my name was Miguel Reyes (close enough to the truth to remember under pressure), and forty-three hundred dollars in cash distributed across four hiding places on my person and in the truck.

I drove east.

I want you to understand something about driving east out of Los Angeles. The city does not let you go all at once. It releases you in stages, like a long handshake from a man who is not sure he wants you to leave. First the freeways thin out, then the strip malls, then the palm trees go from many to a few to none, and then suddenly you are in the desert, and the desert has a sound, papo — the desert sounds like a held breath. I drove through the held breath of the Mojave with the radio off, because the radio was full of songs I did not want to hear, and I let my brain go quiet, and I will tell you, that quiet was the first quiet I had heard in a long, long time.

Phoenix. Albuquerque. Amarillo. Oklahoma City. Little Rock. Memphis. Nashville. Knoxville. The country unrolled under my tires like a long brown carpet getting greener and greener the more east I went, and I started to notice — I did not want to notice, but I noticed — that I had never seen this much of my own country before. I had seen Los Angeles and I had seen TV. That was my America. And now my America was getting bigger, and it had hills, and it had rivers, and it had old men sitting on porches in Tennessee who waved at the truck as I went past, just waved, like waving at a stranger was a thing a person did. I waved back. I felt stupid waving back. I waved back anyway.

Somewhere in the Smokies — middle of nowhere, two in the morning, fog rolling down the mountain like the mountain was bleeding it — I pulled off at a rest stop and I got out of the truck and I stood there in the cold and I looked up. The sky was full of stars. I mean full. I had not known there were that many stars. In Los Angeles you got maybe twenty stars on a clear night. Here there were a million, and they were not arranged in any pattern I had ever been told about, they were just thrown, just spilled across the black, and I stood there in the fog with my breath making little ghost-clouds and I thought, with no warning at all, I thought: Somebody made this.

Then I got back in the truck and I drove on, because that kind of thinking will get you killed in my line of work.

I crossed into West Virginia on a Tuesday afternoon — not the Tuesday Casper had named, an earlier Tuesday, I was running ahead of schedule on purpose because in my line of work the man who is early is the man who is alive — and the country changed again. The hills got steeper. The road started to wind. The trees came right up to the asphalt and leaned over it like they were curious about you. Little towns came and went. Coal trucks. Church signs. CHRIST DIED FOR YOUR SIN, NOT YOUR EXCUSE. I read that one out loud and laughed and shook my head.

Clarksburg. Population, the sign said, around sixteen thousand. I had lived in apartment buildings with more people than that. I came down off the highway into a downtown of brick buildings and church steeples and shuttered storefronts with hand-painted signs, and I drove through it slow with my window down, and I will tell you something, papo — I have never in my life felt so seen. Eyes. Eyes from the gas station. Eyes from the porches. Eyes from the lady walking her little white dog who stopped walking when I rolled past and stood still on the sidewalk and watched me go. I had a sleeve of ink down each arm and ink up my neck and ink on the side of my shaved head, and I was the only brown face I had seen in fifty miles, and I could feel every one of those eyes like a finger laid on me.

It was not hate. That's the thing. I want to be clear about that, because it's easy to make it the wrong shape in your head. It was not hate. It was something more like — surprise. Like I was a deer that had wandered into somebody's living room. They didn't know what to do with me. They didn't know if I was dangerous. They didn't know if I was scared. They just knew I was not from around here, and they were going to have to look at me until they figured out which one I was.

I checked into a Days Inn off the interstate. I parked the truck where I could see it from the window. I locked the product behind two locks and a pillow on top, the way you do. I took a shower. I washed off two thousand miles of road. I sat on the edge of the bed in a towel and I looked at myself in the mirror across the room — twenty-six years old, ink and muscle and dead eyes, a man who had, four days previous, in a kitchen in El Sereno, pistol-whipped a junkie until the junkie's teeth were on the floor in a little white scatter — and the man in the mirror and the man on the bed looked at each other for a long minute, and I did not know what they had to say to each other.

My stomach growled.

I had not eaten since Lexington.

I got dressed, I put the keys in my pocket, and I went out to find some food, and that was the moment — though I did not know it yet, you never know it yet — that my whole life turned over.

Chapter Four

Annabeth

The diner was three blocks from the hotel. I'd walked past it on my drive in and clocked it the way I clock everything: exits, sightlines, who's parked where. It was called something simple — Maple's, or May's, one of those names that was a person before it was a place. Neon sign in the window. OPEN. Twenty-four hours. The kind of diner where the coffee has been on the burner since the Carter administration.

I pushed in the door and the bell over it rang and every head in the place turned. Six heads. An old man in a John Deere cap at the counter. Two construction guys in a booth. A trucker with a paperback. A waitress at the register. And one more head I almost didn't notice at first because she was bent over a table wiping it down, and the angle of her hid her face from me. But the bell rang and she straightened up and she turned around, and she looked at me.

Papo. I have to stop and tell you about this look. Because everything that happened after happened because of this look. Every kindness, every conversation, every moment of grace and every moment of horror that came in the next nine days, all of it lived inside this one look that lasted maybe a second and a half. She turned around with the rag still in her hand and she looked at me, and her face did what every other face in that diner did — it registered surprise, the deer-in-the-living-room surprise. But then her face did one more thing. The other faces stopped at surprise. Hers kept going. It went from surprise to something else — not friendliness exactly, not yet, just — recognition. As if she had been waiting all afternoon to see who would walk through that door, and oh. There he is. And then her face came back to itself, professional, and she gave me the small polite smile that waitresses give, and she said, Sit anywhere, hon, I'll be right with you.

Hon. She called me hon.

Nobody had called me hon in twenty-six years of life on this planet. I had been called many things. Hon was not one of them. I sat down in a booth by the window and I picked up the laminated menu and I tried to read the menu and I could not read the menu, because my eyes were not working, because something behind my eyes was very busy doing something I did not have a name for.

— ✦ —

Her name was Annabeth. I learned this when she came over with the coffee pot and turned my cup right-side up on its saucer and started to pour. The name tag on her apron said it. Annabeth, in slightly faded plastic, with a little smiley face stickered next to it that had been smudged by a thousand washes. She was — listen, I am not a poet, I'm just going to tell you what she was. She was about my age, twenty-five, twenty-six. She had brown hair pulled back in a low ponytail with two pieces escaped on either side. She had freckles across her nose that you could only see if she leaned close to pour the coffee. She had hazel eyes — green when she was looking at you, brown when she was looking past you — and she had the most beautiful pair of working-woman's hands I have ever seen, scrubbed pink, no rings, a small white scar across the back of the left one that I would later learn was from a kitchen burn when she was eleven.

She poured the coffee. She said, Y'all need a minute or you ready?

Y'all. Just me. But y'all. I love this country.

"Cheeseburger," I said. Voice didn't sound like my voice. "And — fries. Thank you."

She wrote it down. She didn't really need to write it down. She wrote it down anyway, the way some people make the sign of the cross before they eat — not because it does anything, just because it is the shape their hand makes. She said, Comin' right up, hon, and she walked away, and I watched her walk away, and I watched the way the apron strings tied in a small neat bow at the small of her back, and I thought — and listen, I have to be honest with you here, I am trying to be honest in this whole thing, that's the only way it's worth anything — I thought a thought that I had thought about a hundred women before, the predator thought, the how-do-I-get-her thought.

And then the thought died. It just died. It came up out of the old part of me and it took two steps into the air and it fell over dead, like a bird that has flown into a window. It was the strangest thing. I sat there in that booth and watched the predator thought die in midair, and a different thought stood up in its place, a thought

I had never had before in my life, and the new thought said, very quietly, You do not deserve to look at her.

I picked up the coffee. My hand was shaking.

She came back with the cheeseburger and she set it down and she said, Anything else? and I said, What time you get off? Because the old me was still driving the car, even if the new me was riding shotgun. The old me knows three plays and only three plays and the third one is always: when do you get off.

She looked at me. She did not look angry. She did not look flattered. She looked tired, the way a woman who has been asked that question two thousand times in her life by men who do not deserve to ask it — she looked exactly that tired.

“I'm gonna stop you right there,” she said. “I don't date customers. I don't date strangers. I'm flattered, I really am. Enjoy your burger.”

And she walked away.

I sat there. The old me wanted to be insulted. The old me wanted to leave a bad tip and walk out and go find a bar and find somebody else to forget by midnight.

But the old me was not in charge of the car anymore. The old me had been driving for twenty-six years and had crashed it into a tree in West Virginia, and the new me, who did not know how to drive, was sitting there at the wheel looking at the dashboard like, ¿qué hago ahora? What now?

I'll tell you what I did. I ate my burger. It was the best cheeseburger I had ever had in my life. I left her a thirty-dollar tip on a nine-dollar check. I walked back to the Days Inn. I lay on the bed. I did not sleep.

I went back the next morning for breakfast. She wasn't on shift. There was a different waitress, an older woman with a beehive hairdo, and I ate my eggs and asked her, casual, when does Annabeth work? and the older woman gave me a long look — a sister-look, a mother-look, a look that said, I know exactly what you are doing, son, and she is too good for you — but she also took a kind of reading of my face, and I think what she saw must not have been the worst thing she had ever seen across that counter, because she said, Tonight. Five to close.

I was there at five.

I sat in the same booth. She came over with the coffee and saw me and stopped about halfway and her face did a small complicated thing that I won't pretend I could read, and then she came the rest of the way and said, "You're back."

"I'm back."

"What can I get you, sir?"

Sir. We had moved from hon to sir. That was a downgrade. I deserved it.

"I'd like to apologize," I said.

She raised one eyebrow. Just one. I didn't know real people could do that.

"For asking when you got off," I said. "Yesterday. That was — that was not a good question. I don't know what other question to ask. I am not from here. I am not — I am not very good at being a person, ma'am. I am trying to learn. I would like to apologize, and I would like to order a piece of whatever pie is the best pie tonight, and I would like to leave you a good tip and go back to my hotel and not bother you. That is what I would like to do."

She looked at me. The eyebrow came down. Her face did the recognition thing again, just a flicker of it, and she said, "Apple. The apple is the best pie tonight."

"Apple," I said.

I had the apple. I left a twenty on a five-dollar check. I went back to the hotel.

The next night I came back for dinner. She brought me coffee without me asking. She did not say much. I did not say much either. I asked her, at one point, very carefully, what was good, and she said the meatloaf, and I said meatloaf it is, and she nodded and walked away, and I ate my meatloaf and I left a normal tip this time, because I was learning that if you tip too much it looks like you are trying to buy something, and I did not want to buy anything. I just wanted to be in the room she was in.

This went on for four days. Four days, papo. I sat in that booth at every meal she worked. I did not flirt. I did not push. I read a paperback I had bought at a CVS — some western, Louis L'Amour — and I drank coffee and I ate pie, and on the fourth day, when she came over to refill the coffee, she stayed standing there a second longer than she had to, and she said, "What are you doing here, Mr. Reyes?"

She had read my credit card receipt. She knew the name I had given. The name was almost mine.

"I am eating dinner," I said.

"In Clarksburg," she said. "What are you doing in Clarksburg."

And here is where I should have lied. The old me would have lied. The old me had eight lies on a shelf for a question like this, ranked by plausibility. But the new me, the one who did not know how to drive, was at the wheel, and what came out of my mouth was: "I came here to do something I should not do. And I would like, instead, if you would let me, to take you to lunch on Sunday."

She held the coffee pot and looked at me for a long, long moment. Long enough that the old man in the John Deere cap turned around to see what was holding up his refill.

She said, "Pick me up at the diner at noon. Sunday. I'm not getting in any car of yours unless I see you in the daylight first."

"Sunday at noon," I said.

She refilled my coffee, and she walked away, and I sat in that booth with my heart doing things in my chest that my heart had not been authorized to do in many years, and on the wall behind the register there was one of those framed Bible-verse plaques that diner ladies put up, and the verse said, in fading gold paint, Be ye kind one to another, and I read it and I read it again and I thought, very far back in my head, the place where the new thoughts were starting to live, I thought: Maybe.

Chapter Five

A Day in the Hills

Sunday came. I had not slept much. I had not eaten much. I had spent two days walking the riverside trail by the West Fork and trying to figure out what a person says to another person when there is no angle, no play, no transaction. I had no script. I had been improvising my way through the diner for four days and I was running out of moves. I wore a clean black T-shirt, jeans, my one button-down over the T-shirt to cover the worst of the neck ink. I looked at myself in the hotel mirror and I thought, this is the most honest thing you can do, and the most honest thing you can do is still a kind of disguise.

She was waiting outside the diner at noon, in a yellow sundress and a denim jacket, with her hair down for the first time I had seen it. Down, her hair was past her shoulders and a lighter brown than I had thought, with little gold pieces in it where the sun hit. She had a big leather purse over one shoulder and she was holding a thermos. She looked at the F-150 and she looked at me and she said, "I'm driving. Get in."

Then she walked over to a Honda Civic from approximately the year I was born — a creature of duct tape and rust and faith — and she opened the passenger door for me, like a gentleman, and she gestured me in. I got in. She got in the driver's side. She started the engine, which took two tries. She put it in gear and pulled away from the curb.

"Where we going?" I said.

"To see something," she said.

And that is all she would tell me for the next forty-five minutes.

She drove us out of Clarksburg, north and east, on roads that got narrower and curvier and more vertical until I was holding the door handle. The trees went from oak and maple to something darker and older. We went up a hollow, then up a ridge, then down into another hollow. We crossed a one-lane bridge that announced its weight limit in a way that made me genuinely concerned about the Civic. We passed a single house every mile or so, and every house had a wave, and she waved at every wave.

I said, "You know all these people?"

She said, "I know about half of them. The other half just wave because that's what you do."

I tried to imagine waving at strangers in Los Angeles. I could not.

She turned off onto a dirt road with no sign. The road climbed for ten more minutes through a tunnel of green so thick the dashboard lights came on. Then we came over a rise and the trees fell away on the right side, and I said, out loud, "Oh."

She had brought me to an overlook. A bald spot at the top of a ridge, where you could see for what looked like fifty miles. Hills folded into hills folded into hills, all of them green, all of them rolling, with a river silver in the bottom of one of the valleys and a hawk turning slow circles over a far-off pasture. There was no sound except wind and the engine of the Civic ticking as it cooled.

She got out. I got out. She walked over to a flat rock at the edge and sat down on it and patted the spot next to her, and I sat down next to her, and she opened the thermos and poured two cups of coffee, and she handed me one, and we sat there.

She said, "This is where my daddy used to bring me. When I was little. He'd bring me up here on Sunday afternoons after church and we'd sit and not say anything, and that was — that was the best time of the week."

She blew on her coffee.

"He died when I was nineteen," she said. "Cancer. Took him four months from the diagnosis. He was a good man. I haven't brought anybody up here since."

She did not look at me when she said that. She looked at the hawk.

I did not know what to say, so for once in my life I said nothing, and we sat there and drank coffee and watched the hawk for what must have been twenty minutes. And in those twenty minutes, papo, something happened to me that I do not know how to describe, and I have been trying to describe it ever since. The fog lifted. Just — lifted. The fog that had been on me since I was twelve years old, the fog inside which I had broken Flaco's elbow and a hundred other men's bones, the fog that was the only weather I knew — it lifted, on a ridge in West Virginia, while a woman I barely knew sat next to me and grieved her father in the silence we were sharing, and underneath the fog was a thing I had not known was there: a young man, twenty-six years old, with a hole in him shaped like a father, who had never in his life sat still long enough to feel how deep the hole was.

I felt it then. The whole depth of it. I felt it and I did not run from it, because I could not run with her sitting next to me, and I think — though I did not know how to say it then — I think that is what grace is. Grace is when somebody sits next to you and you cannot run, and so you finally have to feel.

My eyes got hot. I did not let any of it out. But she saw. Of course she saw. She did not say anything about it. She just leaned over a little and bumped her shoulder against my shoulder, the way a sister does to a brother, and she left it there, just touching, for a moment, and then she straightened up and poured me more coffee.

After the overlook she took me to a little place down in the next town that did barbecue out of a converted gas station. We ate ribs on a picnic table behind the building with our hands. She laughed at me when I tried to use a fork. She showed me a creek behind the gas station where she said she had been baptized, age fourteen, and the water was green and cold and full of tiny silver fish. She drove me down a back road where wild turkeys crossed in front of the car like they owned the place, and they did own the place, that was the joke, we were the visitors. She took me to a cemetery on a hill where her grandparents were buried and she pulled some weeds off the headstones while I stood respectfully at a distance, and the headstones had names on them like Ezekiel and Patience and Wilbur, names I had thought existed only in old movies. She took me, finally, as the sun was coming down, to a Dairy Queen, where she ordered a Blizzard with M&Ms and Reese's together, which I told her was a war crime, and she laughed.

She laughed, papo. She laughed at something I said. I don't know if I can make you understand what that was. I had made many women do many things in my life. I had not, I do not think, ever made a woman truly laugh. Not the real laugh. I had made them giggle, which is a transaction, and I had made them perform pleasure, which is also a transaction, but the real laugh — the kind that surprises the woman herself and comes up out of her like a bird out of a chimney — I had never heard that sound directed at me, and when I heard it in the parking lot of a Dairy Queen in some town in West Virginia whose name I did not even know, with ice cream on her chin, I almost had to sit down.

I felt — and I am going to use a word I never use, because there is no other word — I felt clean.

Just for a minute. I felt clean.

She drove me back to my hotel after dark. She pulled into the lot and she did not turn the engine off, just put it in park, which I understood. I understood every signal she was sending me, in a way I had never understood signals from a woman before, because there was no game being played, the cards were on the table.

I said, "Annabeth, I have to tell you something."

She said, "Okay."

I said, "I have not been honest with you about why I'm here. I came here to do something — a transaction, a thing that is not legal, a thing that is bad, that is going to hurt people I will never meet — and I do not want to do it anymore. I want to not do it. I want to stay here.

I want, if you will let me, to see you again. And again. And after that."

She did not look surprised. That was the thing. I had thought she would look surprised. She did not look surprised. She had known. Of course she had known. A woman like that, she had known the whole time. She just nodded, slow, like a person confirming a thing they had already added up in their head.

Then she looked at me, full on, in the dashboard light. Her eyes were green now, full green, the going-to-tell-you-the-truth green.

She said, "Miguel. I like you. I'm gonna be honest with you because you were honest with me. I like you a great deal. But I have to tell you something that I have told other men before you, and they did not like to hear it, and I am sorry in advance if you don't either."

She took a breath.

"I gave my life to Jesus Christ when I was fourteen years old in a creek behind a gas station. I have walked with Him every day since. He is the love of my life. He is the reason I am the person I am, the reason I am even kind to you, the reason I am sitting here right now and not pretending I never met you. And the thing about loving Him the way I love Him is that I cannot — I cannot — give my heart to a man who does not also love Him. Not because the Bible says so, though it does. Because I know me. I know what I would lose if I tried. I have seen women in my own family lose it. I am not strong enough to be unequally yoked. I'm just not. So I cannot date you. I cannot be your girlfriend. I cannot be the reason you stay in West Virginia. If you stay in West Virginia, you have to stay for a better reason than me."

She paused.

She said, "I'm sorry, Miguel."

And she meant it.

I sat there in that Civic with the engine running and I felt something crack open inside me that I cannot name. Not anger. Anger would have been easier. Something else.

I said, "God hasn't done anything for me. My whole life. I prayed once, when I was nine, when my mother was sick. He didn't show up. He's never showed up. I am not interested in a God who shows up for some people and not for me."

She did not argue with me. She did not preach. She just looked at me with those green eyes and her face was very sad, and she said, very quietly, "He's been showing up for you all week, Miguel. You just don't know how to see Him yet."

I got out of the car. I shut the door harder than I needed to. I walked into the lobby of the Days Inn without looking back. I went up to my room and I sat on the bed in the dark for a long time, and the fog tried to come back, but the fog could not find me anymore — it knocked at the door and it could not get in, because something inside me had changed the lock.

Chapter Six

An Hour Out

The drop was set for Tuesday morning, ten a.m., at an abandoned tipple off a logging road outside a town called Salem, about thirty miles south of Clarksburg. I was supposed to leave the hotel at eight-thirty. I packed at seven. I packed slow. I kept folding the same shirt twice.

I had not seen Annabeth since Sunday night. I had walked past the diner on Monday and looked through the window and seen her working and not gone in, because I did not know what I would say. I had spent the whole of Monday in the hotel room, and on Monday night, around two in the morning, I had gotten on my knees on the carpet next to the bed and I had — I do not know what I had done. I had not prayed. I do not know how to pray. I had said, out loud, to nobody, "If you're real, you're going to have to do this Yourself. Because I do not know how." And then I had gotten up and got back in bed and lain there until the sun came up.

Tuesday morning. I checked out of the hotel. I put the bag in the truck. I put the product, in its hidden compartment, in the truck. I got in. I started the engine. I drove south.

And I will tell you what I thought about, on that drive. I thought about every bad thing I had ever done. I did not want to think about it. It just came. It came in order — chronological — like somebody was playing me a film I had been forbidden to watch my whole life. The fight at school in seventh grade where I broke a kid's nose with a Trapper Keeper. The first time I held a gun. The first time I pointed one. Flaco's elbow. The girl whose name I never learned in the back of a Honda in 2017. The man — I will not tell you about the man, I will not put it on the page, but the man — the man whose face I still see in dreams. All of it. Every one of them. The film rolled and I drove south on a two-lane road through trees coming into their fall colors, and the colors were red and gold and orange, the colors a soul looks like when it's burning, that's what I thought, and I thought, You have spent twenty-six years setting yourself on fire, mijo, and you didn't even notice the smoke.

I was an hour from the drop.

The road went over a small bridge. I pulled over on the shoulder past the bridge. I shut off the engine. I sat there. The truck ticked. A cardinal landed on the hood. Sat there. Looked at me. Flew off.

I thought about Annabeth on the ridge with her father's ghost. I thought about her shoulder bumping mine. I thought about the hawk. I thought about the way she had laughed in the Dairy Queen parking lot. I thought about her saying, He's been showing up for you all week, Miguel. You just don't know how to see Him yet.

I took out the burner phone. I looked at it. I put it back in my pocket.

I started the engine.

And I made a U-turn.

And I drove north.

I was supposed to know where her church was. I did not know where her church was. She had told me once, in passing, when she was telling some other story — a little church on a hill out near Quiet Dell, with a white steeple. That was all I had. Quiet Dell. White steeple. There are about four hundred white steeples within fifteen miles of Clarksburg. I drove north and I drove fast and I prayed — I think it was my second prayer ever, the first one being the carpet in the dark — I prayed, Lord, if You are real, get me to her, You get me to her, I do not know how to find her but You do and I am asking You and that is all I have to give You is the asking. Get me to her.

I do not know what to tell you, papo. I made one wrong turn off the highway, and the wrong turn put me on a road I had not meant to be on, and on that road, around a bend, on top of a hill, was a small white church with cars in the lot and a hand-painted sign out front that said GRACE FELLOWSHIP, ALL ARE WELCOME. I pulled in. The clock on the truck dashboard said 10:54. The sign in front of the church said SUNDAY SERVICE 10AM.

It was Tuesday.

There were six cars in the lot.

I sat in the truck with my hands on the wheel. I thought, Tuesday. There is no service on Tuesday. What is going on. I was about to put it in reverse and try the next steeple, and then a side door opened and a woman came out of the church with a vacuum cleaner cord wrapped around her elbow, and the woman was Annabeth.

She froze.

She saw the truck. She saw me through the windshield. She set the vacuum down on the steps. She walked across the gravel toward me. Her face did not have a name on it. I could not read it. She stopped about ten feet from the truck.

I rolled down the window.

She said, "Miguel."

I said, "I — I did not make the —" and I could not finish the sentence, because the sentence was bigger than my throat. I tried again. "Annabeth. I did not go. The thing I told you about. I did not go. I came here. I do not know what I am doing here. I do not know what — I do not know, I just — I came here."

And here is what she did. She did not make me explain it. She did not ask for the rest of the story. She walked the rest of the way to the truck and she opened my door and she said, “Get out and come inside. Tuesday is when the women clean the sanctuary. Pastor Ron is here. He's a good man. Come inside, Miguel.”

And I got out, and I walked across the gravel beside her, and we went up the steps, and she pushed open the door of the little church, and the inside smelled like lemon Pledge and old hymnals and was so quiet that the quiet was its own kind of sound, and there was a man at the altar replacing a candle, a heavyset man in a flannel shirt and reading glasses, and he turned around and saw me and he did not look surprised either. He just smiled.

He said, “Annabeth, who's your friend?”

She said, “Pastor Ron, this is Miguel. He came a long way to get here. He's gonna need to sit a while.”

Pastor Ron looked at me. Up and down. Tatuajes, tired eyes, two thousand miles of road still on me. He did not blink. He said, “Son, you sit anywhere you want. The whole house is yours. I'll be in the back if you need me.” And he walked back behind the pulpit and through a door, and Annabeth led me to a pew, the third one from the front, and we sat down.

She did not speak. She let me sit.

And I sat there in that empty country church with sun coming through stained glass that had been put up by hands a hundred years dead, and I put my face in my hands, and for the first time since I was nine years old in a hospital waiting room, I cried. I mean cried. I cried the way a man cries who has been carrying something for two and a half decades and has finally been told to set it down. I cried for Flaco. I cried for the man whose face I will not put on the page. I cried for the women I had used. I cried for my mother. I cried for the boy on third base. I cried for the cardinal on the hood of the truck. I cried for every star I had seen over the Smokies and not had words for. And Annabeth did not touch me, and she did not speak, and she did not comfort me, because she was wise enough — wiser than her years, that woman, wiser than mine — to know that some crying is between a man and God, and a third party is in the way.

When I finally lifted my head, my face was a mess. The pew in front of me had wet spots on it. Annabeth handed me a packet of tissues from her purse, and I cleaned myself up, and I looked at her, and she looked at me, and I said, hoarse, "He showed up."

She said, "He always was."

Chapter Seven

Sunday

I stayed in Clarksburg. I checked back into the Days Inn. I called Casper from a payphone outside a Walmart — payphones still exist out there, papo, can you believe it — and I told him I was out. Just like that. I told him the truck had broken down, the product was safe but I was not coming back, and he could send whoever he wanted to come find me, and they could do whatever they wanted, but I was out. He went slow. He went very slow. He told me things on that phone call that I will not repeat. He told me what would happen to me, what would happen to people who looked like me, what would happen to anyone who tried to help me. I listened. I let him say all of it. And when he was done I said, sorry, papá. And I hung up the phone.

I was not naïve. I knew what that phone call meant. I knew that somewhere in Los Angeles a man was making other phone calls now, and that the wires of those phone calls were going to find me, eventually, in a small town where I stood out like a flare. I knew. I had four days, maybe a week. I knew.

But I also knew something else. I knew that I had been dead for a long time, and that I had stopped being dead in a country church on a Tuesday, and that whatever came next, the time I had between now and the bullet — that time was going to belong to me. Not to Casper. Not to the corner. Not to the fog. Mine. For the first time. Mine.

So I stayed. I went to the diner. Annabeth saw me come in and she set down a coffee cup before I sat down. She did not say anything theatrical. She just said, “Pie tonight is cherry. You want?” And I wanted. I wanted everything.

Pastor Ron came to see me at the hotel on Wednesday. He brought a Bible. He sat in the bad chair by the window and he said, “Miguel, Annabeth told me a little. Not much. Just enough. Son, I'm not going to ask you what you've done. That's between you and the Lord. I'm just going to tell you what He has done. You sit with me an hour?”

I sat with him an hour. He read me Romans. He read me Luke. He read me the part about the criminal next to Jesus on the cross — the criminal who didn't pray a fancy prayer, didn't get baptized, didn't earn a single thing, just turned his head sideways at the very last minute and said, Lord, remember me. And the Lord said, Today shalt thou be with me in paradise. Pastor Ron read it twice. He looked at me. He said, "Son, you understand what's happening in that story? You understand the timeline of that story? That man had nothing left. Nothing. He was nailed to a board. He couldn't walk down an aisle, couldn't get dunked in a river, couldn't pay a tithe, couldn't do nothing. All he had was a sentence. And that sentence was enough. You understand what I'm telling you?"

I said, "Yes sir."

He said, "We're going to read this every day this week, you and me. And on Sunday you come to the church. You come to the service. You don't have to do anything. You don't have to walk up. You don't have to raise a hand. You just come and sit. The Lord will do His work in His time. Will you come?"

I said, "Yes sir."

He said, "Good."

Then he stood up to go, and at the door he stopped, and he turned around, and he said, "Son. Whatever's chasing you. You let us help. That's what we do here. You don't have to handle it on your own."

I said, "Pastor, I appreciate that. But this is not a thing your church can help with."

He looked at me a long second. Then he said, "All right. Then we'll just have to ask God to help with it."

And he left.

I spent the rest of the week with her. We went back to the overlook. I met her mother — small woman, sharp eyes, hands like Annabeth's — who looked me over and made me a plate of biscuits and gravy and said exactly two words to me, which were "More gravy?," and that was, Annabeth told me later, an enormous green light. We walked the riverside trail in the afternoons. She showed me the old courthouse downtown. She made me promise to read three books that she said had changed her life, and I bought all three at the used bookstore on Pike Street, and I started one, and the one I started was Mere Christianity, and I will tell you, papo — I read that book by the lamp in the Days Inn until two in the morning, and the man C.S. Lewis was a clever man, a man who had thought himself in and out of his own arguments and come back the other side, and I underlined half the book with a hotel pen.

Friday night Annabeth and I sat on the swing on her mother's front porch and I told her — finally, all of it, no edits — I told her where I was from and what I had done and what was coming for me. She listened without interrupting. She did not flinch. When I was done she sat for a long time, and then she said, "Miguel. I do not pretend I am not scared. I am scared. But I have prayed about this every night since you walked into my diner, and the answer I keep getting is the same answer. I am supposed to love you. So I am going to love you. And we are going to deal with what comes by the grace of God, the same way every Christian for two thousand years has dealt with what came."

She put her hand on top of my hand.

She said, "Whatever happens, Miguel. Whatever happens. He is enough. Do you understand me? He is enough."

I did not, fully, understand her. I would understand her in two days. I would understand her in a way I did not yet have a body for.

— ✦ —

Sunday morning. I put on the same clean black shirt and the button-down. I drove the F-150 to Grace Fellowship. I parked at the back of the lot. I went inside, and the church was full — fifty, sixty people, families with little kids, old men in suspenders, a woman with a walker, a teenager with a guitar tuning up at the front. Annabeth was at the door handing out programs. She saw me and her whole face lit up. She gave me a program. She said, "Sit with me?" and I said, "Sit with you," and we sat together in the third pew, where I had cried five days before, and I held the program in my two hands and I read every word on it, including the address and the phone number and the name of the church secretary, because I did not know what else to do with my eyes.

Pastor Ron preached on the prodigal son. I do not remember everything he said. I remember he said the father in the story was not standing at the gate when the son came home. The father, he said — and he leaned over the pulpit when he said this — the father was running. Running, papo. Running down the road. The son was still a long way off and the father was already running. Pastor Ron said, "That is not how a Middle

Eastern patriarch behaves in the first century. A Middle Eastern patriarch does not run. He sits. He waits. He receives. The fact that this father runs is the scandal of the entire story. The fact that this father runs is the gospel of the entire story. He does not wait for you to get all the way home. He runs. He runs to meet you on the road. He runs because He cannot stand to see His son one more minute away from Him."

Pastor Ron looked at me when he said it. Right at me. Third row. He said, "Some of you came in here this morning with a long, long road behind you. And I'm telling you, son, He has been running toward you the whole way."

And I — listen, I have to tell you, I had not planned to do anything. I had planned to sit and listen, the way Pastor Ron had told me I could. But when he gave the altar call — when the guitar started up soft and he said, if there is anyone here today who does not know Him, who would like to know Him, who is tired of carrying it alone — when he said it, my legs stood me up. I did not stand up. My legs stood me up. And I walked the aisle of that little white church on a hill outside Quiet Dell, West Virginia, and I knelt at the front, and Pastor Ron came down off the steps and he put one big flannel hand on my shoulder, and he said, “Son, do you confess that you are a sinner in need of a Savior?” and I said, “Yes sir, I do.” And he said, “Do you believe that Jesus Christ died for you and rose again?” and I said, “Yes sir.” And he said, “Then ask Him in. Use your own words. He'll know what you mean.”

And I closed my eyes, and I said, out loud, in front of all those people: “Jesus, I am Miguel. You know me. You have been running. Come into my heart, Lord, please, I am sorry, I am so sorry, please come in.”

That's all I got out. That's all I had. I knelt there with my eyes closed and the guitar playing soft and the people behind me singing low, and something — listen, I know how this sounds, I know how it sounds, but I am telling you what happened — something came into the room. Or had been in the room. Or was the room. I do not have words for it. It was warm. It was very, very large. It was personal — that's the part I want you to hear, papo, it was personal, it was not a feeling, it was a Person, and the Person knew my name, and the Person was not angry, and the Person was so glad to see me that I could not bear it, and I started crying again, and I knelt there and I cried and I said gracias, gracias, over and over, in the only language my heart had ever fully spoken.

When I stood up, Annabeth was at my side. I had not heard her come up. Her face was wet. She put her arms around me, and Pastor Ron put his arms around both of us, and the people in the church clapped, and somebody hollered amen, and somebody else hollered amen, and I was in the middle of it like a man who has been pulled out of a river, and that, papo, is what I was. A man pulled out of a river. By a Father who ran.

Chapter Eight

The Parking Lot

After the service I stood in the foyer with her, and the people of the church came up one by one and shook my hand, and not one of them looked at the tatuajes the wrong way, and a little boy of maybe four years old came up and hugged my leg without being told to, just walked up and hugged my leg, and his mother came over and apologized and I said, no señora, please, do not apologize, that is the best thing that has happened to me today, which was funny because so many things had happened to me that day, and we both laughed, and the little boy ran off.

Annabeth and I were the last ones out of the building, after Pastor Ron, who locked the doors. The lot had mostly emptied. There were three cars left — Pastor Ron's, Annabeth's Civic, and my F-150. Pastor Ron got in his car and waved and pulled out, and it was just the two of us in the gravel lot, with the sun on us, and the steeple's shadow falling long across the grass, and the wind in the maples that ringed the property.

I took her hand.

I said, "Annabeth."

She said, "Miguel."

I said, "I love you. I have never said that to a woman in my life, and I am saying it to you now, and I want you to know it is not a closing line. It is an opening line. I want to stay here. I want to live in this town. I want to find work. I want to come to this church on Sundays and Wednesdays and any other day they will have me. I want to take you to the overlook and I want to take you to the Dairy Queen and I want, after a long time of doing those things and earning your trust, to ask you something, and I do not have to ask it now, but I want you to know I want to ask it. That is what I want. That is everything I want."

She looked up at me. Her eyes were green, full green.

She said, "Yes."

Just that. Yes. To all of it.

And I leaned down, and she leaned up, and I kissed her. First time. First real first time of my whole life. Soft, and slow, and not a transaction, and her hand came up and rested against my cheek, and I felt the small white scar on the back of it, and I was, in that moment , I will say it, I was the happiest I had ever been. I am not exaggerating. I had been alive for twenty-six years and I had never, until that moment, been happy. I had been entertained. I had been satisfied. I had been calm. I had not been happy.

In that moment I was happy.

I heard the engine before I saw the car. I heard it but I did not register it. There are sounds you grow up with that your body knows before your mind does, the sound of a low rider with the wrong muffler, the sound of a Crown Vic on a stakeout, the sound of a vehicle that is moving more slowly than it should be moving. I heard the sound. My body heard it. My mind was full of her, and her mouth, and the small white scar, and her perfume, which was lavender soap and nothing else, and my mind did not hear it.

I should have heard it.

This is the only part where I am going to be honest with you in a different way than I have been honest before. I should have heard it. I had been a soldier for fifteen years and the one rule of being a soldier is, you hear the engine before you see the car. I broke the rule. I broke the rule because I was kissing a woman in a parking lot, which is the only good reason I have ever had in my life for breaking it.

The car door opened. Two men got out. I caught the movement in the corner of my eye and I started to turn — too late, much too late — and I saw them, and I knew them, knew them by silhouette, the way you know a relative in the dark. One of them was Pelón. The other was a man whose name I never learned, hired out of Detroit for jobs like this. Pelón had a pistola in his hand already, down at his side, the way you carry one when you are walking to a thing and not from it.

I had time for one thing. One thing only. I had time to put my body between him and her. I did. I turned, I stepped, I put my back to him and my chest to her, and her face was just starting to register the men — green eyes going wide, mouth opening — and I said, very fast, "Annabeth get down," and I shoved her, hard, behind the open door of her Civic. And then the gun went off.

It does not feel like in the movies. It feels like somebody hit you with a hammer. There is a moment where you do not know what happened and you think, did I trip? And then the breath goes wrong, and the breath is the way you know.

I was on the gravel. I do not remember falling. I was looking up at the sky, which was very blue, and there was a single white cloud in the corner of it, shaped like nothing in particular, and I thought, that is a nice cloud. That was my thought. That is a nice cloud.

I heard the car door slam. I heard the engine go. I heard the tires throw gravel. I heard Annabeth screaming my name.

She was over me. Her face came into the sky, blocking the cloud. Her hands were on my chest. Her hands were red. She was saying, Miguel, Miguel, oh God oh God oh God, and her hair was hanging down around her face, and I thought, even then, even with the hammer in my chest, I thought, look how beautiful she is, how did I get to be the one she is bending over, how did this happen to me, what have I done to deserve being looked at by her.

I tried to lift my hand to her face. I did, eventually. It took a long time. I got it up. I touched her cheek. I felt her tears on my fingers.

I said, "Annabeth."

She said, "Miguel, you stay with me, you stay with me, the ambulance is…Pastor Ron! Pastor Ron!...Miguel, you stay with me."

I said, "Annabeth. Listen to me. Listen."

She listened.

I said, "I love you."

She said, "I love you, I love you too, Miguel, please…"

I said, "Thank you."

She said, "For what, Miguel, for what…"

I said, "For helping me find Him."

She broke. She broke and put her forehead down on my forehead and she was sobbing, and I felt her tears on my face, and I felt warm, papo, I felt warm, the way the room had been warm in the church, the same warmth, and I understood…I understood in a way I had not understood before, kneeling at the altar, I had only believed it then, but now I understood it…I understood that the Person was still in the room. Was in this room too. Was the room. Was here, in the gravel parking lot, just as much as in the sanctuary, and was running. Even now. Was running.

I thought of my mother. I thought, mami, you were right. You were right about Him the whole time. I am sorry I did not listen. I will tell you all about it. I will see you very soon.

I thought of the boy on third base. I told him, you can come home now, hijo. He has been waiting on you. You can come all the way home.

The cloud was still there in the corner of the sky. I could see it past Annabeth's hair. It had moved a little. It still did not look like anything in particular. It looked, I thought, like a hand. Or like the back of a man, running.

My eyes closed.

I was not afraid.

There was no fog.

There has never since been any fog.

Chapter Epilogue

What She Said at the Funeral

They buried him in a cemetery on a hill, the same one where her grandparents lay, with the names like Ezekiel and Patience and Wilbur. Pastor Ron preached. The whole little church came. So did her mother. So did some men who had driven from Los Angeles in a borrowed van — friends of his mother's, from the old neighborhood, women in black who had known him as a boy and had wept when she had called them. There was a soldier from Iraq who had grown up on his block. There was a public defender from Los Angeles who had loved a copy of Bless Me, Ultima. There was a young man, maybe seventeen, with new ink on his neck, who had ridden a Greyhound for thirty hours by himself because he had heard the story and had wanted to see the grave.

Annabeth spoke last.

She stood at the head of the grave, in a black dress, with the wind moving her hair, and she said this. I am not making it up. The young man with the new ink on his neck wrote it down on the back of the program, and later he showed me, and these were her words.

She said: "Miguel was in my life for nine days. I want you to hear that. Nine days. Not nine years, not nine months. Nine days. I have been asked, since this happened, by well-meaning people, whether I regret letting him in. Whether I would have been better off if I had been firmer at the diner. Whether God was cruel, to give him to me only to take him."

She said: "I want to tell you what I have come to know. I have come to know that nine days with a saved man is more than a lifetime with an unsaved one. I have come to know that the thief on the cross had even less time than nine days, and the Lord did not consider his salvation a waste. I have come to know that Miguel is, right now, in the presence of his Father — and I do not mean the man who left him on a curb in Los Angeles, I mean the Father who ran down the road to meet him on a Sunday morning in West Virginia — and that he is no longer tired. He carried something for twenty-six years, and on the last Sunday of his life he set it down, and he is not carrying it anymore. He is not carrying anything anymore. And I will see him. I will see him.

Because the same Lord who ran for him is running for me. And He has been running for some of you, too, and you are not as far down the road as you think you are."

She said: "If you remember nothing else of Miguel Reyes, remember this. He was a man with a hole in him shaped like a father. And the Father came, and filled it. That is the whole story. That is every story. That is the only story there is."

Then she sat down, and the wind moved through the maples, and a hawk turned slow circles in the high blue above the hill, and somewhere — I know it like I know my name — somewhere a Father was still running, and a Son was already home, and the road between them was no longer a road at all, but a place where a man had finally been allowed to stop.

— THE END —

www.ingramcontent.com/pod-product-compliance
Lightning Source LLC
LaVergne TN
LVHW010942110826
845149LV00013B/2724